j E-2

MARTIN.

Show and tell.

Date Due			
JUL 07 1982	1296	Л Л	
MAR. 1 5 1984	1380		
APR. 2 6 1984	509		
AUG. 2 8 1984	825		
NOV 2 1 1985	609		
JUN 27 19	643		
FEB 1 8 198	918		
Tristen	5H		
APR 1 9 1998	283		

PRINTED IN U.S.A.

SHOW AND TELL

For
Alana, Barbara, Billie, Bobbie, Bunny,
Cary, Heather, Linda, Lisa, Lynn, Mindy,
Rosemary, Stacy and Tracy

SHOW
and
TELL

by PATRICIA MILES MARTIN

drawn by Tom Hamil

G. P. PUTNAM'S SONS
NEW YORK

by the same author:
BENJIE GOES INTO BUSINESS
THE RACCOON AND MRS. McGINNIS

Text © 1962 by Patricia Miles Martin
Illustrations © 1962 by Tom Hamil
Library of Congress Catalog Card Number: 62-9983
All rights reserved
MANUFACTURED IN THE UNITED STATES OF AMERICA
Published simultaneously in the Dominion of Canada
by Longmans Canada Limited, Toronto

Jeffry liked school. He liked having a desk of his own. He liked his friends and the teacher.

He liked reading and writing and arithmetic and spelling. But more than any of these he liked Mondays.

On Mondays, they had "Show and Tell" at school.

All the boys and girls took something to school to show and tell about.

Unless they forgot, of course.

7

Jeffry had never forgotten.

9

I'M HOME!

On Monday, when he came home for lunch, he looked around the house.

"I have to find something to take to school for 'Show and Tell,'" he said. "I always take something. I never forget. Everyone else in the class has forgotten but me."

"What about taking an autumn leaf?" asked his mother.

"Nope. Autumn leaves are for girls," said Jeffry.

"What about your football?"

"Nope, I took that last week," Jeffry said. "Four other boys took footballs."

He looked in his room. There were lots of things there. There was his book about Indians, his model airplanes, his big box of crayons, and a pair of stilts propped up in the corner. There was nothing there he hadn't taken already. He looked for something different. There wasn't a thing.

He looked in the kitchen. The dog was snoring
under the kitchen table.

"What about taking Bongo?" Jeffry asked.

"Why not?" said Mother.

"If I take him, you have to go too," said Jeffry.

"Oh?" said Mother.

"Yes," said Jeffry, "if we take animals like dogs or cats, the mothers have to go too."

Jeffry's mother hurried to change from her slacks to a skirt.

"How do I look?" she asked.

"Okay," said Jeffry.

Jeffry and his mother and Bongo hurried to school. There were several other mothers there with pets.

"We will ask the mothers to sit in the seats at the back of the room," said the teacher. "I am sure they would like to hear your lessons before 'Show and Tell.' Shall we read?"

Jeffry read first. He left out three words.
The teacher told him what they were.

When he spelled, he missed two words.

"Very good," the teacher said. "You only missed two words."

When they had arithmetic, Jeffry didn't miss at all.

"Wonderful," said the teacher.

Bongo lay on the floor beside Mother and snored.

"We will have to ask that big dog to stop snoring," said the teacher.

Mother whispered to Bongo and he flicked his ear and sat up.

"We will also have to ask the mothers to stop whispering," said the teacher.

You could have heard a feather fall. "We will now have 'Show and Tell,'" the teacher said.

Jill had a cat.

"I will tell you about my cat," she said. "It's a very nice cat. She has three kittens. We will give away two."

Bill had a bird in a cage.

"I will tell about my bird," Bill said. "It is a green parakeet. It talks."

Everyone waited, but the parakeet did not talk.

Anne had an old doll.

"I will tell about my doll," she said. "This is a very old doll. It is as old as teacher. It is over a hundred years old."

Mary had a chicken.

"My chicken is a hen," said Mary. "It lays one egg a day. I have this egg for my breakfast. This is a pet hen. She pecks corn out of my father's coat pocket."

Dick had a clarinet. "I play like this," he said.

"That will be enough," said the teacher. "Very nice, Dick. Thank you."

John had a pot with dirt in it.
"I have a pine tree," he said.
"Right now, it's only a little
seed buried in the dirt, but it will
grow into a tree."

It was Jeffry's turn. He stood up.

29

Just then, the cat jumped out of Jill's arms and
hissed at Bongo. Bongo barked.

The cat ran across the room and Bongo ran after her.

Jill ran after Bongo and Jeffry ran after Jill.

JEFFRY HAD NEVER HEARD SO MUCH NOISE IN SCHOOL BEFORE.

The cat jumped right up on the window ledge and OUT through the window.

SWOOOOOOOOSH, Bongo went too.

"Your mean old dog is chasing my cat," Jill said.
Jeffry leaned out of the window.

"Bongo won't hurt your cat," he said. "He was
only playing. LOOK, he's stopped chasing your cat
already. SEE? They're sniffing noses. Bongo likes
cats. He was just tired of school."

The teacher rapped on the desk. "Shall we all go back to our seats? Jeffry, it is your turn, I believe."

Jeffry stood there with nothing to show and tell about.

"Too bad," said the teacher.

Jeffry thought for a minute. "I have something to show and tell about," he said. "I have my mother."

"Unusual, but acceptable," said the teacher.
"Will you stand beside Jeffry, if you please?"
"Certainly," said Mother.

"I will tell about my mother," said Jeffry. "She can throw a ball straight. Sometimes she can catch. She's a good cook, and she doesn't always have to have her own way."

When "Show and Tell" was over, everyone went
home. Bongo was waiting for Jeffry on the front
porch.

At supper that night, his father said, "How was everything at school today?"

"Okay," said Jeffry. "We had 'Show and Tell.' I took Bongo, but he only stayed for the lessons."

"How was spelling?" asked his father.

"He can't spell," said Jeffry.

"I mean YOU," said his father.

"I was okay," Jeffry said. "I missed two words."

"How was arithmetic?" asked his father.

"Okay," said Jeffry. "I was best."

43

"He took me for 'Show and Tell,'" said Mother.

"How were you?" asked Father.

"Okay," said Mother.

"Best in class," said Jeffry.

"Thank you," said Mother. "You make me feel proud."

Jeffry thought about Mondays. "When we have 'Show and Tell' NEXT Monday, I won't have anything as good to show and tell about. What'll I take?" He looked at his father.

"Don't look at ME," said Father. "I'm a working man."

Jeffry looked at Bongo.

Bongo thumped his tail on the floor.

"I'll take second best," said Jeffry. "I'll give Bongo one more chance."

The End